Sophie Washington Hurricane

Written by
Tonya Duncan Ellis

Books By
Tonya Duncan Ellis

Sophie Washington: Queen of the Bee

Sophie Washington: The Snitch

Sophie Washington:
Things You Didn't Know About Sophie

Sophie Washington: The Gamer

Sophie Washington: Hurricane

Table of Contents

Chapter 1

Lightning

Kablam!

"Ahhhhhowwwww!!!" my little brother Cole's screams combine with our dog Bertram's howls, as a blinding light flashes near the backyard. The hair on my arms stands on end. We zoom to the kitchen race car fast.

"Mooom!" I call.

Thunder booms. I cover my ears to stop the ringing. My mother, wild-eyed, joins us.

"It's lightning!" she cries, pulling Cole and me in for a group hug; Bertram shivers in the middle.

Outside, rain pounds down in sheets. The power cuts off.

"Great," says mom, as she stumbles through the blackness to the pantry to find candles and a lighter.

For about three minutes, we huddle together quietly in the dimly lit room.

"What do we do now?" Cole breaks the silence.

He edges way too close to me, and I have the urge to shove him off like I usually do, but I feel sorry for my little brother because if I'm scared, I'm sure he's terrified.

Poot!

"Ewwwww! You are so nasty, Cole!" Now I do push my little brother back. Leave it to him break wind at a time like this.

"Excuse me," he says.

My mother starts giggling.

"I can't believe you're laughing, Mom!" Pinching my nose, at the sulfurous odor I stamp my feet.

The lights flick back on, and I squinch. Bertram barks and wags his tail happily.

I exhale, then sharply breathe back in a few seconds later, when we hear a clatter coming from the garage.

"Wait here, kids," our mother cautiously moves toward the door that leads outside.

"Be careful," I warn.

A minute later, she comes back, and my father follows. He's wearing green scrubs from his dental office, so he must have had to fill cavities today. As usual, he looks calm even though the rest of us are freaking out.

"Daddy!" Cole and I cry, nearly knocking him down with our hugs.

The thunder was so loud we didn't hear the garage door open.

"Did you see this?" he asks holding up a burnt plastic square that looks like a lunchbox someone set on fire.

"Lightning must have struck our back fence, and the volts burned up the electrical sockets to the sprinkler system," Dad explains. "This box was blown across the wall clear to the other side of the garage when I came in."

"Thank goodness it didn't start a house fire!" Mom responds.

She starts moving around the kitchen to finish dinner, as things get back to normal, and I sit down to catch my breath. I see Cole sneaking his handheld video game out to play his favorite Video Rangers game. The rain has slowed down to a drizzle. I absently stroke Bertram's black, curly fur and look out the window at water gushing from our sprinkler system.

I've always felt it was like the *Animal Planet* channel here in our home near Houston, Texas. We've had huge buzzards on our roof, wild pigs in our front yard, and last year, we actually saw an eight-foot-long alligator in our subdivision when we were riding our bikes. Those things were crazy, but lately, it seems as if the natural world it taking over even more. My friend Mariama and her family had to ride down their neighborhood in a kayak last year when rain water flooded their house, and Dad's dental office filled with almost two feet of water too.

Lately, we've had Noah's ark-like rain storms, and according to the weather reports, it's going to get worse.

"Turn on the news and see what they are saying," says Dad.

"A Category 2 hurricane is headed toward Corpus, Christi, TX," says the newscaster. "We are watching the storm closely and will keep you updated on all developments."

"What's a hurricane?" asks Cole. "Isn't Corpus Crispi where Granny Washington lives?"

"It's Corpus Christi, Silly" I say smacking his head.

"A hurricane is a huge storm that has heavy rain and lots of wind," explains mom. "Remember when we had Hurricane Ike a few years ago and all those trees in our front yard fell down?"

"He was only two then, and he's still a baby now," I laugh.

"At age 11, it's not like you're a senior citizen," mom replies.

"I'd better call your grandma to see what her plans are," Dad pulls out his cell phone.

He waits a few seconds with the phone to his ear, then starts dialing again. "That's funny," he frowns. "The phone keeps dropping my calls. Your grandma keeps her phone charged at all times, so I wonder if the reception there is just bad because of the storm."

Ten minutes later, Dad still hasn't reached our grandma, and we all start to worry.

"I hope the storm doesn't wash Granny Washington away," Cole exclaims. "Where is she?"

Chapter 2

News Flash

"The storm isn't going to wash grandma away," I say laughing. "She's probably just in an area with bad Wi-fi or something."

"Let's hope so," says Mom. "Come on guys, let's sit down for dinner."

Dinner tonight is something I like, thank goodness, baked chicken, green beans, and mashed potatoes. My mom's cooking is really good, but my parents are health nuts, so most of the time we have things like salad, broccoli and cabbage on the menu, which Cole and I hate. Cole sometimes tries to hide his veggies, like the time he put his Brussels sprouts under his seat cushion. Mom found out a couple of days later when it started smelling like something died in the kitchen. He got in Video Ranger level 100 trouble for that.

Mom keeps the lights off, and we eat by the glow of the candles she got from the pantry. Dad says grace and thanks God that we are all safe from the terrible rain storm and that our house didn't catch fire.

"Will the hurricane be able to come here to Houston?" I ask.

"They say we will probably get a lot of rain, but the heavy winds will cause the most damage in Corpus Christi," Dad replies.

He looks anxiously at his cell phone on the counter to see if our grandmother has called him back.

"Don't worry, Daddy," I say trying to soothe him. "I'm sure Granny Washington just went to the store or something and turned her phone off."

After dinner, Cole and I settle down in the family room to finish our homework. Since I'm in the sixth grade I have way more work than he does in the second grade, which I think is completely unfair. We both have it worse than other kids in our neighborhood because we're students at Xavier Academy, a private school that stresses academics. The worst part about going there is that I have never gotten to ride on a school bus like other kids do, except for field trips. Mom drives us to school every morning. And we also have to wear boring school uniforms; polos and skirts for me, and polos and khakis for Cole.

"You're still studying?" Cole asks after fifteen minutes go by. "I'm already done with all my work."

"That's because I'm in middle school and you're in day care," I retort. "You never have any real homework."

"Do too," he comes back. "I'm just better at getting mine done. And second grade is NOT day care."

Cole pulls out the family lap top and pretends to study vocabulary words on Quizlet when our parents come in the room. I know that he is actually playing a video game he has downloaded, but I don't bother to say anything to Mom and Dad. Since he's the smallest one in the family, my little brother gets away with everything. This past Spring he gave up video games for 40 days for Lent, but still kept sneaking to play them, and when my parents found out, not much happened to him. Let me do ANYTHING wrong, on the other hand, and I'm in for it.

An hour later, I finally finish my math and science homework and watch a TV show with the rest of the family. Midway through the program, there is an announcement from the weather man.

"The Corpus Christi storm has been updated to a Category 4 level, and the governor has issued a mandatory evacuation for the area," says the announcer. "All residents are advised to leave the city as soon as possible. The storm is expected to make landfall in three days."

Dad jumps up and tries to call grandma again from his cell phone, and then from our house phone, but still gets no answer. He dials a couple of her friends' houses, and they don't pick up either.

Chapter 3

Road Trip

"I may need to take a trip to Corpus," says Dad.

"What?!!" my mother jumps up from the couch. "You can't head into an area where there is a hurricane."

"It's not like my mother not to answer her phone," he replies. "Maybe something is wrong. I don't want her to get stuck down there when the storm hits. If I leave now, I could pick her up this evening and bring her back here with us."

Corpus Christi is about a three-and-a-half-hour drive from our house in Houston. Cole and I go there to visit our grandmother for about a week each summer. Our grandfather died when we were smaller, and grandma lives alone in the house my dad grew up in. We like spending time with Granny Washington and playing in the sand at the beach. Last year, she even took us to Padre Island, which is a town a few hours from Corpus that has even nicer beaches with white sand. We visited a water park and went on a boat tour to see dolphins. I wanted to swim with them, but grandma said she'd seen the old movie *Jaws* too many times and didn't want to risk us getting eaten alive.

"Can I go with you, Dad?" asks Cole.

"No, Squirt, you need to stay here to go to school tomorrow. I think I will head out this evening and then come back early in the morning with your grandma."

Mom looks upset, and she doesn't say anything else as my father heads upstairs to pack his overnight bag. My parents don't argue much, but I can tell when they are not happy with each other, and it doesn't look like Dad is her favorite person right now.

"Who is on dish duty tonight?" she asks.

I look at Cole, and he looks at me. Mom taught us both to rinse the dishes and load the dishwasher a few months ago, and both of us try to get out of doing it whenever we can.

"Since neither of you is stepping forward, why don't you both help out," Mom orders. "I need to go speak to your father for a minute."

I move over to clear the pans off the stove.

"Bring over the dirty dishes from the table," I instruct my little brother, as I head to the sink.

I then start scraping leftover food in storage bowls to put into the fridge.

"Yuck, what are you doing? That is gross!!!" I exclaim a few minutes later, when I see Cole setting the dinner plates on the floor, and Bertram slides over to lick them.

"It helps them get cleaner faster," he replies, as I shoo the dog away and pick up the dishes.

"Now I know why mom doesn't want you in the kitchen by yourself," I say. "It's a wonder we aren't all in the hospital."

Dad and Mom come back downstairs, and we give him a hug as he heads back out to the garage.

"Please be safe, sweetie," says Mom tearing up.

"Don't worry it's still light out now, so I should arrive in Corpus about an hour after nightfall," assures Dad. "We will head back home as soon as we get up in the morning to beat the traffic."

"The road may be crowded with people trying to get out of Corpus Christi, and here you are driving into it," Mom frets.

"I've got to get my mother out of there before it is too late," he replies.

We all stand at the door and wave as my father drives away. Hopefully he will come back soon.

Chapter 4

Rain, Rain, Go Away!

Drip, drop, drip drop.

A fine mist of rain splashes on the car window as we roll down the road.

"Get your feet off me," I complain, shoving Cole over toward his side of the back seat.

"I'm not on you, you're on me!" he elbows me back then slams his tote bag onto my backside.

He looks cute and cuddly, but Cole can be a major pain in the rear. My parents say I acted the same way when I was his age, and that I have matured since I started sixth grade a few months ago, but I don't believe it.

"Cut it out back there, or you're both in trouble!" my mother warns. She turns on the car radio to drown out our squabbling. I know she is nervous that Dad is still not home.

Last night he called to let us know he made it safely to our grandmother's house. She has an older flip phone and it hadn't been working well because lines were down from the storm. They are on their way back to Houston and should make it before we get home from school.

Cole starts to hum tunelessly, and I am very happy when we pull up to my school.

"See you later Mom!" I hop out the car as soon as it stops moving, and Cole follows right behind.

"Have a nice day kids," calls Mom. "Love you!"

The scent of chalk, old books and wet umbrellas hits my nose as I enter the hallway, and dodge the jostling bodies of 200-plus middle schoolers. I smile as I get closer to my locker.

Though Xavier Academy is not my favorite place in the world, it's fun to be with my friends every day. I spot my besties Chloe Hopkins and Mariama Asante and our other friends Toby Johnson and the Gibson twins, Carly and Carlton. In the middle of the group is Valentina Martinez, a girl I can't stand.

"Hola! Did anybody see the new routine our cheer squad was practicing last week?" she says, tossing her shoulder length, black hair and doing a shimmy. "We're performing it at the next basketball game, and it's going to be so Lit."

"Awesome," says Chloe. She and Mariama hang on Valentina's every word. It's no secret that they want to try out for the cheer squad in a few weeks. I'm not that into sports, and I definitely don't want to prance around cheering for a bunch of silly boys. Besides, I would rather be part of the action than the atmosphere at a game.

Ever since her BFF Maria Garcia moved a couple of weeks ago, Valentina's been pushing her way into our friend group. Her constant adding of Spanish words to every conversation makes me gag. I'm so irritated thinking about Valentina that I don't pay attention to where I'm going.

"Watch out!"

Nathan Jones, a boy I've known since fifth grade, zooms around the corner with a mason jar in his hand and clear plastic science goggles on his face. Nathan is wearing a white lab coat, and hopping in front of him is a ginormous gray-green frog.

"Eeeeek!" I scream in shock, unable to move.

"Grab him, Sophie! I need that frog to finish my science experiment!!" Nathan calls.

Water sloshes out of the jar as Nathan and the frog get closer. Then he steps in the puddle and starts sliding. He's running so fast that he can't slow down.

"Oh no!" I cower to avoid him, but as he swerves, Nathan dumps the water from the jar on my head. We ram into each other, ending up in a jumbled heap on the floor then the frog leaps over us, croaks and heads down the stairway.

Click!

"That was hilarious!" laughs Valentina snapping a picture on her cellphone. "I can't wait to post this."

"Don't you dare!" I struggle to my feet, and try to snag her phone, but she shuffles away.

"Look everybody!" she shrieks, skipping over to the growing group of kids.

I quickly glance at Nathan. "Are you OK?"

"Yeah, just bummed that Exhibit A of my experiment got away," he says standing and rubbing his head. Nathan is one of the smartest kids in the sixth grade, and a good friend. He had surgery on his leg last year when a bully pushed him down in the hallway, so he is always careful not to injure it again.

"Let me see those pictures," I shove my way into the group, and all my friends are bent over their phones, laughing at the photos Valentina took of me and Nathan.

We're tangled up on the checkered school floor like a Twister game gone wrong. My mouth is open in a scream, and Nathan's eyes are bulged out. The most embarrassing is the shot of the frog leaping over our heads.

"Nathan wishes he could jump that high on the basketball court," jokes Toby Johnson.

"It looks like Mr. Toad and Sophie are smooching," giggles Valentina, her brown eyes twinkling. "Like mi abuela always says, Sophie, you need to kiss a few frogs before you find your prince."

I want to slap her but don't say anything. At least she put the pictures on SnapShot so they should be gone by tomorrow.

"Very funny, Valentina," says Nathan. "If anyone happens to see Mr. Toad, please let me know because I need him to finish my science project."

"Sure thing, bro," Toby gives him a fist bump.

"I'm sorry for laughing, Sophie," says Chloe. "I'm glad you guys weren't hurt."

"We're fine," I say, as I wring more water from my plaits.

Valentina changes the subject, and brings out some churros to share that her grandmother, or abuela, as she calls her, made. The sweet cinnamon scent makes my stomach growl, but I don't eat any. Next, Valentina invites Chloe and Mariama to meet her in the gym after school to practice cheers.

"I thought we were going to study for our English quiz together in aftercare," I tell Chloe.

"Could we do it tomorrow?" she asks. "I really want to get that new cheer routine down before tryouts."

"The quiz is tomorrow," I answer. "And you're the one who asked me to help, you, but that's OK, forget it."

"Bueno, let's walk to English class together!" Valentina links arms with Chloe and Mariama, and I walk two steps behind.

By the time my mom pulls up to get me after school, I can't wait to go home. The rain starts falling again as soon as we slip into our seats, and my bratty brother immediately begins his antics.

"Why did the iPad go to the dentist?" he jokes "It had Bluetooth."

I stare out the window and shrug when Mom asks me about my day. There is no need to tell her my feelings. She always takes everyone else's side. I already know what she'd say: "You're being too sensitive, Sophie. Give other people a chance."

But I know that Valentina is as fake as monopoly money, and I'm going to make sure that everyone finds out.

Chapter 5

Home Sweet Home

When we get home, I pet Bertram on the head, and make my way to the fridge.

"There's nothing to eat in here," I moan.

"Sure, there is," my mother looks over my shoulders. "I see apples, and grapes, or what about making a peanut butter and jelly sandwich?"

"PB and J is for five-year-olds," I grumble.

"Can we get smoothies and fries from Sonic?" chimes in Cole. "I want some good food."

"Well then, you need to get a good job," counters Mom. "because I am not paying to eat out for snacks again, when we have plenty at home."

"You always get all that healthy stuff," I say. "There is nothing we like."

"You kids are too spoiled for words," says our mother. "But I guess I have helped create two monsters by giving you everything you ask for all the time. Figure out what you are going to eat for snack and get started with your homework, or wait until we eat dinner if you don't like the snack food we have."

She walks out of the room and I keep my mouth shut. I can tell when I am pressing my luck. Mom and Dad say that Cole and I are spoiled all the time, but I don't see it. There are plenty of kids who get way more than me. Take my cell phone, for example, I had to beg for it for nearly a year, while all my friends already had one. And it seems like Chloe and even that big mouth Valentina talk about shopping in the mall nearly every weekend. I don't want that many new clothes, and we wear uniforms to school every day, but still.

I grab some cheese and crackers then sit down to do my homework at the kitchen table. I hear mom turning on the family room television.

"Hurricane Pedro is rapidly making its way up the coast," says the announcer's voice. "It may land sooner than projected, and we expect heavy rainfall in the Houston area for the next several days."

Mom picks up our phone and calls our dad. "When are you getting home, honey?" she asks as soon as he answers. Cole and I listen expectantly.

She nods her head and smiles at his response.

"They are in downtown Houston now," she tells us.

"That means Granny will be here soon!" Cole and I jump up and down excitedly.

We love it when our grandmother visits us. She cooks our favorite foods, plays board games with us for hours and always buys us nice gifts and gives us money before she returns home. When she worked, Granny Washington was a newspaper reporter, and she loves to tell us interesting stories about the famous people she interviewed from all around the world.

"Go straighten up the guest bedroom, Sophie," says Mom. "And make sure you two didn't leave any of your toys in there."

I trudge off to do as I'm told. Of course, Cole sits near the edge of the couch drawing, and doesn't make one move to help. I glance back to see if my mother will tell him to come with me, but no such luck. I don't complain this time because I'm so happy that my grandmother is on her way here and that she wasn't trapped in Corpus Christi by the storm.

"We got out of the coastal area right in the nick of time," says Dad once he and Granny Washington finally make it home. "There was so much traffic it took us six hours to get here rather than the usual three and a half."

"Hopefully the storm won't be as bad as they predict," says my grandmother, pulling my brother and me in for a hug.

"Though the circumstances aren't the best, I'm sure happy to see my little sweeties," she says, pinching both our cheeks again. "I have special treats for you both."

"Awesome!" We both hop up and down excitedly.

I pull open the large bag she brings and grab a pink cowgirl hat, and a cute checkered shirt to match.

"Cool! Thanks so much, Grandma! I've always wanted a hat to wear to the rodeo and "Go Texan" day at school."

Cole gets a matching blue, boy-sized hat that he immediately puts on, and a lasso to swing.

"I'm a rootin' tootin' cowboy!" he shouts.

Great. Now he'll have another crazy get-up to put on.

Cole loves to dress up as wacky characters like pirates, magicians, and Star Wars Jedi whenever he can.

"And who do we have here?" Grandma asks looking at Bertram, who eyes her warily.

She hasn't visited since we got our dog. Bertram followed us home from school one day, and when we found out that his owners were looking for a new home for him, he joined our family. We named him Bertram because the way his fur is black all over his body and near his neck, but white in front makes him look like he's wearing a suit and tie like the butler from the old *Disney* show Jesse.

Grandma pulls out a package of animal crackers from her purse.

"Grrrrrrrr," Bertram tries to sound ferocious.

"Here you go, Poochie," she coos, rubbing his head and offering him a treat.

A whiff of the goodies changes Betram from big bad wolf to lap dog in a second. He licks grandma's fingers and gulps down the cookie. Then he wags his tail and starts sniffing her shoes.

"You'd better watch out, Grandma, 'cause Betram tried to eat half the shoes in the house when we got him," warns Cole.

"Once he gets a taste of these old loafers, he might start sticking to dog food," Granny Washington laughs.

"One or two cookies should be alright, but not too many," Mom adds. "The vet says the dog will get sick if he eats too many sweets."

As grandma catches us up on her life in Corpus Christi, I snuggle close to my father on the couch. I am glad that my family is here safe in our home sweet home.

Chapter 6

Vámanos

It was hard to leave for school the next day knowing that my grandmother was here. Usually she comes during school breaks and holidays, and we get up late and eat a big breakfast of homemade pancakes, bacon and eggs with her. But since it's Wednesday we have to follow our normal school routine.

"Won't the children be hungry?" Granny Washington questions my mother when she sees me grab a piece of fruit and a container of yogurt and Cole gulp down a bowl of cold cereal.

"This is what we normally eat during the week, and the kids are fine," Mom says picking up her purse. My mother used to be home most mornings after she dropped us off at school, but now she works three or four days a week at our father's dental office. We get home later in the afternoons sometimes now that she's working. But my parents also agreed to let me get a cell phone so they can call and check up on Cole and me when we stay at aftercare, so I'm happy with that. For a while, I was the only kid in my class who didn't have a cell phone, which made me feel even more babyish than Cole.

"See you later, Grandma," Cole pecks Granny's cheek, and I give her a big hug, breathing in the scent of lavender she wears.

"Make sure to take your umbrellas, because it looks like it's still raining," she says.

"I'm so tired of this rain I could scream," complains Mom as we pull out of the driveway.

"I'm getting tired of it too," says Cole. "Since it's been raining all week, we haven't been able to go outside for recess."

Mom drops us off early and I make my way to the gym to hang out before class starts.

Most of the boys from our class are playing basketball. Valentina, Mariama and Chloe are demonstrating the cheer routine they were working on after school.

Boom Chicka Boom!
Shake the Room!
Rockets Got That Zoom, Zoom, Zoom!
We Will Get the Win Tonight!
Come on Xavier Fight, Fight, Fight!

"Not bad, ladies," says Nathan Jones, stumbling over from the basketball court. He is usually the last one picked for any team, but he still loves to play.

"I see you haven't found Mr. Toad yet," I say, spying the empty mason jar near his backpack on the floor.

"Yeah, the janitors said they saw him after school, but he slipped by them."

"Hola, Sophie, Nathan," Valentina comes to greet us. "How'd we look?"

She is being "extra" as usual, and is wearing red, glittery shoes a la Dorothy from the *Wizard of Oz* with her school uniform. I'm surprised she didn't fall and break her neck doing that routine with heels on.

"Just great," I crack a fake smile. "I'm sure you'll all make the team."

"Let's go practice our splits, ladies, before the warning bell rings," says Valentina. "Want to join us, Sophie?"

"No thanks," I say, turning around and heading to the hallway. "I forgot I need to get to class early."

"Ok, Adios," says Valentina cheerfully.

My friends follow her like zombies.

See you. Hope you don't get knocked out by a wayward basketball.

"What's that moving in the corner?" says Valentina. "Hey, Nathan, is that your frog?"

"Yes, I think it is," he says, peering through his glasses at the green blob bouncing around the gym. "I need to stop it. My project is due soon and it's too late to start something new."

"What is the experiment on?" I inquire.

"How many breaths per minute the frog takes," he answers. "Mr. Toad has had me running around so much that I ought to measure my own breathing."

"Don't worry, I'll get it for you!" calls Valentina. Suddenly, she triple-flips across the gym Simone Biles-style, and throws a duffle bag over the frog to stop him.

Everything comes to a standstill in the gym. All the kids start applauding.

"Way to go Valentina!" cheer Chloe and Mariama.

"Wow! Thank you," Nathan exclaims after she brings the frog to him. "That was unbelievable."

"De nada," Valentina says shrugging her shoulders.

I, for one, can't believe this is happening. The entire school is in love with this phony.

If you ask me, Valentina is muy rude. Why does she always have to take over everything?

I was sure wrong thinking of Nathan as a smarty pants. Even he can't see through Valentina's "Miss Sweetness" act. I wish she would take Dora the Explorer's advice and vámonos.

Chapter 7

Deep Waters

Grandma Washington is a sight for sore eyes when I get home from school that afternoon. Not only did I have to listen to all my friends rave about Valentina's great churros and tamales during lunch, but everyone was also all abuzz about her gymnastics stunt.

"How was your day sweetie?" Grandma gives me a big smile and sets a plate of sugar cookies on the table.

"Cookies! Om nom nom nom!" Cole grabs three cookies and shoves them in his mouth at once, like the Cookie Monster character on Sesame Street.

"Move out of the way, silly," I say as I nab two.

Grandma pours us both glasses of milk, and we tell her about our school days.

"We had lots of fun in art class," says Cole. "We're studying famous artists, and our teacher is having us copy some of their paintings. I'm doing Pablo Picasso."

"I'm sure that will be interesting," Grandma remarks.

Cole is really talented in art and has won about five blue ribbons for his paintings and drawings at the Houston Livestock Show and Rodeo. He's only seven years old and can paint horses, steer, cowboy hats, bluebonnet flowers and just about anything like a pro.

"Not much happened in my class," I say. "Some kids are worried about the rain because they don't want their houses to flood again like they did last year."

"Maybe school will close," Cole says, looking on the bright side.

"The hurricane hit in Corpus Christi this morning, shortly after you children went to school," says Grandma. "And there does appear to have been quite a bit of damage, so I'm grateful your father came and got me. I haven't been able to reach my friends there to see how they are doing. I'm praying they will be fine."

"When is it going to stop raining around here?" Cole asks.

"Hopefully soon," Grandma replies. "The weatherman says the storm clouds have moved up to this area for a few days."

After dinner, my parents turn on the television again, and Cole and I get great news.

"There is flooding in southwest Harris County," says the announcer. "Highway 288 is impassable in many sections, so county schools will be closed until further notice."

"Yay!" Cole and I start to dance around the family room.

"I hope we don't get water in your dad's office again," frets Mom. Last year when we had flooding, water rose up to her knees in his dental office, and he had to work in a building across the street for a few months. Since then he's moved to the second floor of a medical building.

Within a half hour, it starts to pour again. Our backyard looks like a lake, and I hear frogs croaking. "Maybe you can take us to Game Shop tomorrow, Grandma, and get a new video game, since we don't have school," suggests Cole.

"From the looks of the roads, you won't be going anywhere tomorrow," says my father frowning out the window. On the television, I see scenes of water covering people's cars as they try to make their way home through flooded areas of our city.

I start to get nervous.

"Dad, what's going to happen?" I ask as I move toward the stairs to go get ready for bed.

"Don't worry, Pumpkin," he answers. "It'll be alright."

Chapter 8

The Office

In the morning I wake to a sound I haven't heard for a few days. Silence. I smile when I see that the rain has finally stopped.

Since we don't have school, maybe Cole and I can play outside on our scooters, or shoot some baskets on his goal.

I pad downstairs in my house slippers.

Both my parents and grandma are in front of the television again. And they tell me to limit my screen time!

"What are we going to do?" my mother turns to my father.

"Let me try to get a hotel room," he responds. "All the roads are closed, and we can't leave town."

"What's going on?" I ask. "Why are all the roads closed?'

"Every major Houston highway has flooded," responds Grandma. "They say the levees may break in your subdivision, and it might flood in the house, so the authorities are telling us to leave here for a few days. We're trying to decide where to go."

"What are levees?" I ask.

"Walls built to keep rivers from overflowing with water," Grandma explains. "If the water gets higher than the levees, it spills out on the roads and they flood."

Dad sets down his cell phone. "It's no use. All the hotels in Houston are booked."

Mom paces the kitchen floor, and Bertram starts whimpering to go outside.

"Why can't we stay here and just go upstairs if it floods?" I ask. "The water can't get all the way up there, can it?"

"We don't know how long the high waters will last," Dad explains. "There could be a chance of us getting stuck in the house and running out of food, or even getting electrocuted if water gets in the electrical outlets."

"Mmmm, mmmm, mmmm," whines Bertram. I shush him.

"I've also heard that flood waters have sewage, snakes, alligators and other scary things in them," adds Mom.

I feel something wet on my slipper and jump.

"Yeeck! Bertram just peed on my shoe."

"I guess you had better take him out back before he makes his own flood in here," chuckles my father, grabbing some paper towels.

"Come on, boy." I don't get mad at him because he *was* asking to go outside.

When I return from taking Bertram out back, my parents give me some news.

"We're going to your father's office," shares Mom. "It's on the second floor of a medical building that has a backup generator to keep the power from going out. There's also food in the medical center cafeteria we can eat in case we can't get to the store."

"It's yucky hospital food," says Cole, joining us in the family room.

"With the way things are looking, we will be lucky to get it," says my father showing us pictures of crowds of people lined up at our neighborhood grocery store from a social media post on his phone.

Things get frantic as we quickly pack, and move furniture, photo albums and other valuable items upstairs. About two hours later, we load up our car and head out.

"I would have loved to cover a story like this when I was a reporter," says Granny Washington, looking out the window at the water covered areas. "But at this point in my life I don't want to be in it."

"Look at all those cars!" Cole points at the parking lot at the Mega Food Town grocery store. Every parking space has a vehicle in it, and there is not one grocery cart to be seen.

"I don't want to think about what it's like inside that place," marvels Mom. "I've heard there are at least two thousand parking spaces in this lot."

"Look at all that water!" Cole peers out the back window of Dad's SUV.

"It's starting to cover part of the road," answers Dad. "We are getting out of here in the nick of time."

We near the exit to our subdivision.

"Thank goodness," sighs grandma.

"Oh no" I exclaim. "We forgot Bertram!"

Chapter 9

Dog Out of Water

"We can't leave my dog!" cries Cole.

"He's not just yours, he's mine too," I start to argue. "And if you hadn't been trying to steal my duffle bag when we were loading the car, I would have noticed he wasn't here."

"Did not."

"Did too."

"Calm down, children," Mom commands. "Will we be able to go back to get him?" she looks at our father.

"Please, Daddy, he'll starve," I beg.

Dad turns and makes a U-turn near the drug store at the subdivision entrance, and we drive back toward our house.

"Woo-hoo!" Cole and I cheer. "Hurry up, Dad."

"I can't drive too fast or we'll skid," our father says. "Just sit back and be quiet."

I can't believe how quickly the water is rising. You can't see grass on either side of the road anymore. We've got to get out of here! A line of cars is making their way out of the neighborhood, and it starts to rain again. My chest feels tight.

"We are heading in the wrong direction," Grandma shakes her head.

As soon as we pull up to our house, my father rushes out of the car.

"Bertram! Here, boy!" he calls.

"Hey Bertram!" I rush out of the back seat to help.

"Wheet wheet!" Cole whistles a call.

Water splashes under my feet in the driveway.

"Come on, boy, it's time to go."

Both the back and front yards are empty, and there is no sign of our dog anywhere in the house either. All our neighbors are gone.

After fifteen minutes of searching, Dad turns to us, "We've got to get going, kids."

"But we didn't get our dog!" Cole starts to tear up.

"I know, and I feel terrible about it, but this is a serious situation. We need to get out of the neighborhood before we are stuck here."

"What if an alligator or snake gets him?" I cry.

"We have to just hope for the best, sweetheart, but we need to leave, now."

My brother and I trudge back to the SUV, and everyone is quiet as we make our way back out of our neighborhood. I can't believe we lost Bertram. He must be terrified.

"At least he has his dog collar on," Grandma reassures us. "Someone will help him find his way home."

The road outside our subdivision is more difficult to drive through than Dad expected. We move at a turtle's pace behind lines of cars for nearly two hours. Normally, it takes about fifteen or twenty minutes to get to Dad's office.

"I've got to use the restroom," whines Cole.

"Hang on just a little while longer," soothes Mom. "We're almost there."

"Don't think about a running faucet," I tease.

"Cut it out, Sophie," says my father curtly.

At an intersection, we see cars turning around.

"The water in the road looks too deep to pass," Mom exclaims.

"We can do it," says Dad determinedly.

He slides in a lane behind an 18-wheeler truck. The truck plows through two-feet deep water and Dad follows closely in the path it makes.

"We're going to float away!" I close my eyes tight.

At least three feet of water gushes up near our car windows.

"My goodness!" Granny Washington exclaims.

It feels like the longest five minutes of my life, but we finally make it through the high water to Dad's office, which is on a dry street, for now.

"Excuse me, but I gotta go!" Cole runs down the hall to the men's restroom, as soon as my father opens the building door.

"I don't know how much more excitement I can take," says Grandma Washington stretching out of the vehicle.

Hopefully, we can stay put for a while.

Chapter 10

The Visitors

Dad has a kitchen area in his office, and Mom and Grandma walk there to check what is in the cabinets and fridge.

"We have ramen noodles, a few cans of soup and plenty of bottles of water back here," Mom tells grandma. "Plus, all the food that we packed and brought from home."

"A few of the restaurants nearby looked like they were still open when we drove up," says Dad. "We can always go to them for a hot meal, if the cafeteria is closed, as long as the road outside stays clear."

"Where will we sleep?" I ask my mother.

"In here," she points out the examining tables.

"That's where people get their teeth cleaned!" I protest, glancing at the sterile, white environment.

"Once we put our sleeping bags and comforters on top they will be fine beds," Granny Washington assures.

The Wi-fi is working in the office, and I get out my cell phone, while Cole happily starts playing his video games. I text all my friends and find out how they are doing. Nathan and his family drove to Austin last night and Chloe and Mariama are safe and dry at their homes. Toby says his house hasn't flooded so far, and he and his parents and brother are staying in a hotel.

"I swear, we could be up to our eyeballs in water and these kids would be just fine as long as they have their electronics," Mom shakes her head.

Dad settles into a soft chair in the waiting room for a short nap. For the next half hour, we relax.

Buzzzzzzz. Buzzzzzz.

I jump.

"What's that annoying sound?" asks Cole, taking a breather from his game.

"It sounds like the door buzzer downstairs," Mom replies, looking up from her book.

"Who would want to get their teeth cleaned in the middle of a hurricane?" Cole questions.

"I doubt anyone is coming for a check-up," I snap, setting my cell phone down.

"I hate to wake your father up, when he's sleeping so peacefully," says my mother. "Let me go check out the peephole, and you guys stay here."

We sit expectantly while she inches down the stairway to the front entrance of the building.

"What if it's a robber?" asks Cole.

"If it is, they can't push or shoot their way in because the door is made of steel," I answer. "And I remember Daddy saying there's an alarm system and some security men who work in the building too."

"Let's not be negative, children," says Grandma. "I'm sure it's just a delivery person or something."

Mom comes back and shakes Dad's shoulder.

"There's a family at the door, looking for shelter," she says.

He rubs his eyes. "How many people are there?"

"An older woman, a preschooler, and a little girl around Sophie's age. They say they live a couple of blocks over, and their house and car flooded. All the neighbors have evacuated and they have no other family in the area."

"Let me meet them," Dad answers, putting on his shoes.

Five minutes later, my parents return to the office lobby with an elderly Hispanic lady wearing a blue housecoat, a little boy sucking his thumb and holding a dirty Snoopy stuffed animal, and Valentina!

Chapter 11

More Than Meets The Eye

I am in shock.

Oh no! Not "Miss It." Being trapped in Dad's office with Valentina is almost worse than riding through the flooded streets of Houston.

My parents start making introductions.

The old lady is Valentina's grandmother, Martina, and the younger kid is her little brother Hector.

"Gracias for your kindness, Señor," says Mrs. Martinez, tearing up. "We are so grateful to you for letting us stay. Our home is filled with water, and our friends left. We lost everything! We have nowhere else to stay and did not want to go to the shelter."

"How did you find this place?" I blurt out.

"We walked from around the corner, and saw the light on, and thought maybe we could buy some food in the cafeteria or sleep in beds in the medical building," the older lady replies.

"I didn't know you lived in this neighborhood, Sophie," says Valentina.

"We don't. This is where my dad works."

"You two know each other?" Dad looks at me.

"We're in the same class in school," I reply.

"Valentina got a special scholarship to attend Xavier Academy last year," says her grandmother proudly.

I watch as Valentina blushes.

"I'm hungry, Abuela!" whines the younger boy.

"There's plenty of food in the kitchen, and you're more than welcome here," says Mom, breaking the awkward silence. "We have some extra cots in the other examining room you can use to sleep on this evening, as well."

As my parents show Valentina and family around our new living quarters, I race to my phone to text my friends about this horrible turn of events, then decide against it. They all like Valentina and will be happy she is safe.

"Maybe you can share your bunk with Valentina this evening, Sophie," suggests Mom. *No way Jose am I spending the night with that braggamuffin!*

"If it's OK, I'd rather stay in the room with Cole," I answer.

Mom raises her eyebrow at that strange response because usually I'm trying to get away from my little brother.

I walk into the kitchen area to find Valentina and her brother eating steaming bowls of Ramen noodles, while her grandmother knits a blanket.

"Your family is so kind to let us stay here," the older woman says, smiling at me. "We are very grateful."

I nod my head not knowing what to say.

Hector loudly slurps his soup, then accidentally pushes his bowl off the table, splattering the remaining liquid all over the floor.

"You silly boy," scolds Valentina. "Look at the mess you made!"

Hector starts to sob noisily and rubs his runny nose. I wish that we had let the buzzer ring and not answered it. Loud piercing noises drive me crazy. My parents tell me that I used to cry a lot when I was smaller, but I can't believe I was this annoying.

"It's fine," Granny Washington comes to the rescue. "Here are some paper towels. Just wipe up the mess from the floor and it will be as good as new."

As order is restored, Hector starts to suck his thumb and cuddles his Snoopy dog.

Valentina looks mortified. *At least she has the good sense to be embarrassed.*

"Where are your parents?" I ask.

She wriggles about uncomfortably and doesn't say anything.

"Mami and Papi are in jail," answers little Hector.

"Jail?" I blurt out in surprise.

"Valentina's parents were arrested because their working papers to be here in the United States expired," explains Martina. "They were released and returned to our home in Mexico City two years ago, but wanted the children to stay here in America for a better life, since they were both born here. I am lucky I was able to get my green card a few years ago and can stay as long as I want."

"How old is Hector?" I ask in surprise. "When is the last time you saw your mom and dad?" He couldn't be more than four years old. That means he probably barely remembers his parents!

"That's enough, Sophie," says my mother interrupting the conversation and eyeing Valentina sympathetically. She looks like she is going to cry.

I feel bad now about thinking all those mean things about her. I can't imagine not seeing my parents, or even Cole, for two years.

I thought she was just a bubble headed cheerleader always trying to be in the limelight, but she has some serious issues. It seems like there is more to my classmate than meets the eye.

Chapter 12

New Friend

Before I can ask any more questions, Valentina storms out of the kitchen space and heads to the waiting area of Dad's office. I decide not to follow her.

"Excuse her rudeness," apologizes Martina. "Not having her parents around has been very hard for my granddaughter. She doesn't like to talk about them much with strangers, and Hector doesn't understand since he was just two years old when they had to leave America."

"Please don't apologize," says Mom. "I'm certain any child would be upset if they were separated from their parents under such circumstances. I'm sorry that my daughter asked such intrusive questions. Sophie, why don't you go see how Valentina is doing?"

I trudge to the waiting area like cement is on my shoes, wondering what I'm going to say. Why didn't I stay in the back room earlier with Cole and his video games?

Valentina is watching a news show in the room where my father is leaning back in a chair, snoring.

"Sorry for asking so many questions about your parents," I say.

"It's fine," she responds quietly. "It's just harder being without them with all this going on. When Papi and Mami where here we never had any troubles. But now things are always going wrong."

The newscaster is pointing out firefighters in boats rescuing people from their houses.

"That looks like the back section of my subdivision, near the soccer fields!" I exclaim. "We are lucky we got out when we did. I sure hope Bertram is OK!"

"Who is Bertram?" asks Valentina.

"He's our dog. We packed up to leave so fast we forgot him, and when we went back to check on him we couldn't' find him anywhere."

"That's terrible!" Valentina exclaims. "Hopefully he found shelter somewhere. I was so scared when all that water got into our house. We went to the second floor and we weren't sure if we could get out. Some policemen rescued us, and told us to walk over to this block where there was no flooding. All my toys and clothes are gone."

Her voice starts breaking again, and I try to think of something to cheer her up.

"It's a good thing you and your family members made it here to safety. And think of the bright side, you'll get to get brand new toys and clothes once all the waters die down."

"My clothes are from Goodwill as it is," sighs Valentina. "And Abuela had to get my school uniforms from a special resale they had at the end of the year last year, so I'll have nothing to wear! We don't have the money to buy new things."

"If your family is so low on money, how can you be on the cheer squad?" I ask. "I thought those cheer uniforms are really expensive."

"Maria gave me her old ones when she moved, and the school lets me go to cheer camp on scholarship, since I'm the captain," she explains, starting to sniffle again.

Now I feel awful. Even though I don't get to shop to the mall as often as I like, Cole and I never have to stress out about what we are going to wear.

"Don't worry, Valentina," I say moving closer to her. "I'm sure there will be something we can do to help. You and I are about the same size, and I have extra school uniforms you can wear. And Chloe is the tallest girl in our class, so she may have some leftover things she's outgrown that you can have. As much as she shops, they are probably all practically new."

"Thanks, Sophie," says Valentina, wiping her eyes.

I switch the television to the Disney channel to take our minds off the storm, and we watch a sitcom.

It's funny how my feelings about Valentina have changed in just a few hours. Earlier in the day I considered her my worst enemy, but now I feel like I have a new friend.

Chapter 13

Homeless

My other classmates are still safe when I text to check up on them later in the afternoon. They think it's cool that Valentina and I are hanging out at my Dad's office.

We make a tent with some extra covers in the examining room we will be sleeping in this evening. Mom has found some microwave popcorn in the kitchen area and says we can have a movie night and watch some cartoons that are coming on in the waiting room before we go to sleep.

After we get tired of watching television and looking at our phones, Valentina teaches me some of the cheer tryout routines.

"You're a really quick learner, Sophie," she says. "Have you ever taken any dance classes?"

"No," I answer. "I do go to Cole's basketball games every week in the winter, so maybe I have learned some things from watching the cheerleaders there."

"You'd be a great flyer since you're so tiny," she answers. "You should try out for the squad."

I've always thought cheerleading was silly, but doing the routines is kind of fun. It takes more coordination to learn the moves then I thought.

If I wasn't worried about Bertram I would actually be having a good time during the hurricane. We're out of school, we're getting to spend extra time with our parents and grandma, and I've made a new friend.

Hector is wearing Cole out with a ball he found to play catch with.

"Hike, hike, score!" he yells running down the hall for the twelfth time.

"Was I this hyper when I was four?" Cole asks huffing up to my father.

"That hyper times ten," Dad laughs.

Cole convinces Hector to watch him play video games for a while, and Valentina and I join our grandmas and my mother in the kitchen area.

Mom is looking out the window.

"The rain is slacking up, and the newscasters are saying the worst of the storm is over. We just have to wait to see if the water floods our neighborhood once the river crests."

"When can we go home?" I ask.

"I'm not sure sweetie," she answers. "They say the river should get its highest in another day or two. If it doesn't rise above the levees and cause any more flooding in our subdivision, I'm sure they will clear us to go back home."

Valentina looks stricken.

"One of our church members will let us stay with their family until we find a new place," her grandma consoles her.

"And you can always come to our house whenever you want," I offer.

Mom looks at me surprised, with pride.

"That's very generous of you, Sophie, and very true Mrs. Martinez." Mom replies. "You all are welcome to our home anytime."

"That's if we aren't flooded out as well," cautions Grandma Washington. "Remember that we are still under an evacuation order too."

Grandma's reminder prompts my mother to check her cell phone for social media updates on the storm from our neighborhood.

"So far, there is no water near our house," she reports. "One of our neighbors has returned and is watching for looters on his porch with his shotgun. It seems that robbers have been going around the city breaking into homes after people leave from the flooding."

"That is just terrible!" my grandmother exclaims.

I start to get scared again. Things feel safe and cozy here in Dad's office, but much more is going on outside than I imagined.

"Will someone break in our house, Mom?" I scoot close to her.

"I doubt it, dear," she reassures me, "but if they do, we have the alarm system on, so the police will catch them, and even if someone did take some of our belongings in the house, we are all here together and that is what matters most."

Bertram's not with us, I think. But I don't say anything because Cole and Hector walk in the room looking for cookies and I don't want him to get upset.

Valentina and I practice our cheer moves until dinnertime, when we all head to the medical center cafeteria to get hot meals. It's kind of chilly in the eating area, so I wish I brought my sweater, but the mingled smells of fragrant casseroles, fries, soups and other foods make me forget being cold.

Valentina and I choose pasta dishes, and Cole and Hector order burgers and fries.

"This is much better than all the vegetables we eat at our house," my brother grins stuffing his face.

"We may need to have a few extra salad-dinner nights to get your nutrients up when we go home," Mom jokes running her hand over his head.

One of the medical center administrators comes over to our table while we are eating.

"How's everything going, Dr. Washington?" he inquires.

"Fine, Jim, I trust you and your house are safe?"

"Yes, things are dry in our part of town," Jim answers, "and some of the roads are starting to clear. We are thinking about opening up portions of the office in the next day or two."

He and my father continue talking off to the side, and my mother and grandmother exchange glances.

Everyone finishes eating, and our group makes their way back upstairs to Dad's office.

"It was good to get some fresh air," says Valentina's grandmother once we close the door to the waiting room.

"Yes, it kind of feels like we are hideaways or in an alternate universe up here," says Mom.

"Well, we should be able to get lots of air tomorrow," says Dad. "Because the administrators want us out of the office. The roads are clearing and they want to allow patients to come in for medical emergencies."

"But we're homeless, Dad!" I cry. "They're saying on the news that we can't go back into our subdivision for at least two days."

"Think of it as an adventure, Sophie," says Dad. "We'll be heading somewhere out of town."

Chapter 14

San Antonio

After some discussion and phone calls, my parents and grandmother announce that we will be driving to San Antonio tomorrow morning to stay at a resort hotel, and the Martinez family will join us.

"I cannot repay you for this," protests Valentina's abuela when my father shows her a picture of the hotel, which includes a golf course, and a water park area with water slides and a lazy river pool.

"Consider it a gift from us for all your troubles," he says. "Having you here has made this entire experience much less traumatic for our children. With you and your grandkids in the office it's been more like a mini vacation for Cole and Sophie than a natural disaster."

It has been nice having Valentina to talk to, and though he's been grumbling, I think Cole likes playing the big brother role to Hector.

Mom brings in some towels and wash cloths she finds in the supply closet and takes me and Valentina down to a locker room area on the other side of the medial building that has showers.

I feel like I am in a summer camp as I wait for Valentina to finish up in the shower area then go in to take my turn after she finishes. Once the boys are taken down to the showers to get cleaned up, we settle down on sleeping bags in the waiting room to watch a movie.

While we curl up on the carpet, Mrs. Martinez stoops over and lays warm, knit blankets on top on me and Cole.

"A gift for you, niños," she says.

"Those blankets are so beautiful!" protests my mother. "and you worked so hard on them, you could probably sell them rather than give them to these kids."

"I finished these this afternoon," she says. "I can make others later. Please accept them as a small repayment for your kindness."

My new blanket is so soft and snuggly, that I drift off the sleep in the middle of the movie. I wake to mom and Granny Washington urging me and Valentina up to the examination room for the night.

They have taken our tents down, and laid comforters on top of the examination tables to make them feel more like mattresses. I'm glad I'm really sleepy because it's kind of creepy falling asleep on a mat where people have their teeth drilled.

"Good night, Valentina," I say to my new friend.

"Good night, Sophie," she replies groggily.

I guess the busy day has her worn out too.

In the morning we dress quickly, then rush to join everyone else in the kitchen area. There are muffins to eat and orange and apple juice bottles to drink.

"Our SUV seats eight, so there is room for everyone," says Dad. "But since the storage area in the back is a little tight, we'll leave all the bedding and things we don't need here in the office."

"I can hold my new blanket with me in the car," I say, holding it close.

We all pile in, ready for a new adventure. My heart starts racing after we drive off, remembering how the water came up to our windows on our way to the office, but the roads are dry now. It doesn't even look like we had a hurricane.

Evidence of the storm becomes clearer as we make our way down the road. Pools of water cover the grass, and some trees have toppled at the roots because of the sodden ground.

"Whoa! Check that out, Sophie!" exclaims Cole, pointing at a house with the roof blown off.

We make it to San Antonio at lunchtime and stop at a diner to get something to eat.

"You kids are out of school today?" asks our server as she passes out menus.

"We are from Houston, and had to leave our home," Dad explains.

'We've seen a lot of evacuees here the past couple of days," the waitress replies, before taking our drink orders. "I will give you a couple of minutes to look over the menu."

It's funny being thought of as an evacuee. I look over at Valentina, and have a weird feeling in my stomach thinking about how she has lost everything. *I am glad that so far, our house is safe.*

Chapter 15

Natural Bridge Caverns

Our hotel rooms won't be ready until 4 p.m., so Dad suggests we do some sightseeing before we head to the resort.

"I've always wanted to take a tour of Natural Bridge Caverns," suggests Granny Washington.

"That sounds like a fun outing," says Mom.

"What are caverns?" asks Cole.

"Cavern is another word for caves," my father explains.

"Will there be bats there?" I ask.

"Let's hope not," Mom replies.

"I had a friend who visited there a few years ago, and I don't remember her mentioning seeing any bats," Granny Washington answers.

The first thing I notice when we enter the visitor center to buy our entry tickets to the cavern are bat shaped stuffed animals, on a sales rack.

"Look at these cute pajamas!" Valentina points out some pants with cartoon bat designs all over the fabric.

"I thought there were no bats in here, Granny?" I ask her, with my eyebrow raised.

"There are occasionally sightings of bats during cave tours, but it is rare," says the cashier.

"I don't want to see anything living in the cave," I reply.

"Me either," echoes Valentina.

My parents buy all our tickets and we line up to enter the cave.

"You stay close to me, Hector," Valentina's grandmother instructs her little brother.

"Are you sure you want to go in, Mrs. Martinez?" asks Mom. "You could get a cool drink by the play area or we could get Hector tickets to do the zip lines while you wait for us."

"I'm in pretty good shape for climbing since I walk every day and do a lot of labor at my job," says Mrs. Martinez. "It will be a good experience."

Coles starts teasing as soon as we enter the dark cave.

"Nah-nah, nah-nah, nah-nah, nah-nah, nah-nah, nah-nah, nah-nah, nah-nah, Batman!"

"Stooop!" I shriek, in terror.

Valentina giggles nervously.

"Darkness falls across the land, the midnight hour is close at hand, creatures crawl in search of blood, to terrorize y'all's neighborhood," Cole continues his teasing by repeating the lyrics from Michael Jackson's "Thriller," song.

"Mooom," I whine.

"Children be quiet!" she hisses. "Cole go to the end of our group away from Sophie and Valentina."

Dark, humid and spooky, with a damp, musty smell, this cave would be the perfect spot for a Halloween haunted house.

"It's illegal to touch the rock formations because it will harm them," warns the tour guide. "There is actually a fine for doing so."

She goes on to describe the different rock formations within the cave. "Stalagmites form from the floor, and stalactites are the formations you see hanging down from the ceiling of the cave."

"Fascinating!" exclaims Granny Washington, borrowing Dad's cell phone to snap a photo.

Water drips on my head and I jump, scared that a wayward rock will crumble down.

I look over at Hector, and he is sucking his thumb contentedly and doesn't seem to be a bit nervous. I guess ignorance is bliss.

"Those formations that resemble dried egg yolks were made from petrified bat guano, or droppings," says the guide.

"Ewww!" Valentina and I exclaim, shaking.

I don't think I'll stop being petrified until we get out of here. We climb up some steep areas and wind around a curve. Just when I think we're getting closer to the exit, the tour guide slows things up to take group photos of the twenty or so people taking the tour. Many of them are from our subdivision in Houston.

"We got out just before our neighborhood started flooding, but the water started receding before it got to our house," a man tells my Dad.

"The water still hasn't reached our area of the neighborhood yet," replies Dad after congratulating him. "This is certainly an experience."

It's time for our group to gather under a huge stalactite for a cool pic.

"Come on y'all, gather 'round," Mom calls to us. Everyone lines up, and the guide starts arranging us.

"How many are in your group?" he asks.

"Eight," Dad responds.

"I only count seven here," the guide counts down the line. "Who's missing?"

Cole!

Chapter 16

Little Boy Lost

"Wait! My little brother isn't here," I say to Valentina.

"He was just in line behind me a second ago," says Mom. "Where can he be?"

I realize that I haven't noticed him since he was bugging me when we first entered the cave.

"He was right beside me about five minutes ago," shares Dad.

"Cole!" I call.

"Hey, little guy," shouts one of the other tourists in our group.

We search the general area for a couple of minutes, then Hector takes his thumb out of his mouth and speaks.

"Cole was looking at the bat poop."

"The bat guano we saw is about a five minute walk back on the trail from where we are now," says the guide. He pulls out his Walkie Talkie and calls for backup.

"We can continue along the trail, and another guide will join us with your son," he tells my mother and father.

"I'm not leaving this area until I see my child," Mom takes a seat on a nearby bench.

"Too bad we didn't have that attitude when the Cole was with us," scolds Granny Washington. "Someone should have been watching that child more carefully. He seems mature, but he's still a little boy."

Mom bites her lip. I know she is angry but doesn't want to get into an argument with Dad's mother.

"I'm sure he'll turn up soon, Mrs. Washington," says Valentina, trying to be helpful. Her grandmother stands beside my mother and touches her shoulder.

The rest of the group continues on through the trail and we wait in the humid area for Cole.

If they don't find out he's hurt, I'm going to kill him. It is downright eerie in this cave, and if he hadn't been up to his usual shenanigans, we would be out of here that much sooner.

Sweat is dripping down my forehead ten minutes later, when two other guides and Cole walk up the path.

"You had us worried to death, son!" cries Mom pulling him into a tight hold.

"I'm sorry, Momma. I stopped to see the bat guano, and when I looked around everybody was gone."

"He got turned around and headed the opposite way in the trail toward the entrance," the guide explains.

"Well, you owe your parents an apology, young man, scaring us all like that!" reprimands Granny Washington. "But I sure am happy to see you!"

By the time we make it to the cave's exit, the rest of the tour group is long gone.

"I don't ever want to see the inside of a cave again!" I declare.

"I liked it," says Valentina's grandmother. "The rock formations were muy bella."

"I was too worried about becoming a bat snack to pay attention to what the rocks looked like," I say.

"It was a cool adventure," says Valentina. "I wonder if they have special tours for Halloween?"

"If they do, count me in!" says Cole. "Same bat time. Same bat channel."

Chapter 17

Hurricane Break

We spend the next day at the hotel resort and have a great time swimming in the waterpark during the day, eating brisket and baked beans for dinner at the on-site restaurant, and making s'mores by the campfire that evening.

"My family has never had a vacation this nice, Sophie," says Valentina as we float down the lazy river to watch a flick and float movie showing on an outdoor screen by the pool.

"Thanks again for bringing us. I'm having so much fun! It almost feels like we haven't lost our home."

"It's like Hurricane Break!" I laugh. "I'm glad we could come here with you guys too." Then I get quiet, because I don't know what else to say. My family has been travelling to this resort at least once a year since I was about six. I don't remember ever thanking mom and dad for bringing us.

Cole and I share a room with Granny Washington that evening, and The Martinez family is in their own room. I'm so tired from all the excitement that I fall asleep as soon as I hit the pillow. In the morning we all get back together for a huge buffet breakfast before driving home to Houston.

"The water has gone down in the levees near our subdivision, so we are out of danger of having our home flooded," Dad says after checking for updates on his phone.

"Yay! We can go home now!" cheers Cole. "I hope my dog is coming back too."

"There wasn't any dog food around, so Bertram probably went to another house in the neighborhood," I guess. "They will figure out he is ours because he has his collar on."

Before we hit the road, Dad decides to get gas for our vehicle. All the gas stations near the hotel are out of fuel.

"There must be fuel shortage because of the storm," Dad figures. "If we don't find anything soon, we may have to go back to the hotel, because we don't have enough gas to make it back to Houston."

Lines at the next two gas stations, wrap around the block. My heart beats fast when I see a police officer with a rifle standing near one gas pump. Finally, we are able to find a gas station with a shorter line in a neighborhood a few blocks from the highway.

"I hope the fuel situation isn't the same as this when we get back to Houston," Mom says.

It's decided that that Martinez family will stay with us for a few days when we get back in town, until they get situated. I am happy because I'm having a great time hanging out with Valentina. It's kind of like having my own same-age sister. We get along really well, and it's been lots of fun learning the cheers she's taught me. Now I think I may try out for the squad with her and my other friends.

Chapter 18

Sophie Strong

When we step through our front door, I feel like Dorothy must have felt when she returned to Kansas from the Land of Oz.

"There's no place like home!" I cry flinging myself on the den sofa.

"Get your bags unpacked, help Valentina and Hector get settled in your rooms," instructs Mom. "Mrs. Martinez, you can share the guest room with my mother-in-law. We will bring in a pull-out bed."

"I hate to put you out, so," she protests.

"Nonsense, it will be nice to have some company who is my age," Granny Washington reassures her.

Dad's dental clinic is still closed for a few days, so he decides to drive the Martinez family to their house to assess the damage the next morning.

"Can I come too, Daddy?" I ask. "I want to help."

"I don't see why not," he replies. "Just make sure you wear your rain boots to make sure your feet don't get cut or wet. We'll be wearing special protective suits and masks to keep us safe during cleanup. And you'll need to follow all our instructions, or we will have to make you stay in the car."

"Yes, sir."

I grab my boots and follow Dad, Valentina and Mrs. Martinez into the SUV. Mom comes along too. Granny Washington stays home to watch Hector and Cole.

"I'm anxious to get to my house, but scared of what we'll see there," says Valentina, as we drive down the highway. "Water was really getting high when we left, and we didn't have time to pack up much of anything."

"Dios will take care of us, whatever we find, just as he always has," reassures her grandmother.

Mockingbirds sing, and cotton ball clouds fill the powder blue sky as we pull into the Martinez's driveway. It's hard to believe this bright, sunny landscape was the scene of a flood crime just a few days ago.

"We don't have a car," says Mrs. Martinez. "so we didn't have to worry about that flooding."

Once she gets the key in the door she struggles to get it open, but it won't budge. "I don't know what could be the matter with this lock," she says.

"Let me help," says Dad, using all his strength to shove it open.

We all look in astonishment at the huge mess.

The carpet is covered with at least an inch of mud, and the walls have mold on them that's as high as my waist. To the side of the door is a wooden coffee table that must have been what was blocking it. Everything is helter-skelter, with kitchen items mixed in with clothes and the living room furniture. The room smells like the Cole's tennis shoes after a basketball game.

"My whole life is in ruins!" Mrs. Martinez struggles to keep from falling.

Valentina picks up a ragged doll from the ground and starts to shake.

"There, there," my mother pats my friend on the back and hugs her grandma. "Don't you worry about anything. We're here to help."

"We've got to get to work, clearing everything out of the house," Dad takes control. "Everybody, put your suits on."

We look like astronauts wearing the hazmat suits, plastic gloves and masks my father says he picked up at the home improvement store this morning.

"Can we save anything?" Mrs. Martinez asks.

"I'm afraid not," my mother answers. "Most of these things have mold damage. You can make up a listing of what you've lost once we're done to send to the government, or your insurance company, for a possible refund check."

"We don't have flood insurance," Mrs. Martinez cries.

"Don't cry Valentina," I say, patting my friend's shoulders as she struggles to hold back the tears again. Mom gives her another big hug then she and Dad start working.

I follow my parent's lead and begin loading the thick garbage bags with belongings that we place on the curb. After about a half hour, people arrive in neighboring houses and start clearing them out as well.

We are mostly quiet as we work.

"Need any help?" a man peeks his head in the open front door around 11:30. "My name is George Randal. My sons and I came to Houston from Austin with our church group to help in any way we can."

Mr. Randal and his two college age sons, Skip and Clint, help us haul things out from the house for the next couple of hours and pull the refrigerator out to the curb, before we stop for a lunch break.

"You've been doing a great job, girls," says Dad, as we munch on tacos from a truck that drove through the neighborhood. The men that work on the truck are friends of Valentina and Mrs. Martinez, and attend their church. Valentina and her grandmother catch up with the food vendors on what is going on in their neighborhoods while we eat.

"I'm glad I can do something," I answer. "I feel so helpless! I can't believe all this has happened."

"I think you're stronger than you think, Sophie," says Mom coming up to give me a squeeze. "You're doing the best thing that anyone can under the circumstances, and that's being here for your friends."

Chapter 19

Watch Dog

Though it's great to be back in our house, we are sad that after three days, we still haven't seen any signs of our dog Bertram. At Cole's urging my mother has checked the local shelter two times already. And we've put signs up all over the community. Our neighbors are back in their houses, and they haven't seen our puppy either.

"Just be patient, love," says Granny Washington. "He'll turn up soon."

She's heading back to Corpus Christi this afternoon, and the Martinez family left to stay with some of their church members yesterday.

"It was terrible going through the storm, but I'm glad we were able to be with you and your familia," said Valentina, giving me a hug before they said goodbye. "See you at school next Monday."

"Ok, see you!" I replied.

Schools are closed for another week to give families time to recover.

With the help of Mr. Randal and his sons, we were able to clear everything out of the Martinez's home, and strip down the molded areas from the walls and floors. Now they have to wait for a check from the government to see if they'll be able to repair the damage to their home or will need to move.

Bike riding down the trash-laden streets with my brother I realize how fortunate we are that our house did not flood. There's old furniture, appliances and other waste heaped up at the curb of every home, just a few streets over.

"Look at that huge pile of wood!" Cole exclaims, excitedly. "We could build a tree house with that!"

"Don't get near it because it may have sharp nails or other things in the pile that can harm you," I warn, feeling like my mother.

We rush through the back door to the kitchen when we go back home to see Mom and Granny Washington sitting at the table with a visitor.

An older man is seated to the side of my grandmother, holding a leash in his hand. I see something moving near the man's chewed up black shoes.

Ruff! Ruff!

Up pops Bertram from a lounging position, almost knocking me over as he slathers my face with licks!

"Bertram! Hey Poochie!" Cole gives the dog a bear hug. "Where have you been?"

"He found his way to my back patio right after the flooding started," says the man. "Your precious 'Poochie' has been enjoying himself, eating all my food and chewing on my shoes. He kept me company during the storm, since I didn't have the good sense to leave when everyone else did."

"Thanks so much, Mr. McEwan, for taking the time to find out where Bertram lives and bringing him back to us," says my mother. "The children have been just devastated without him."

Mr. McEwan stays to chat for about a half an hour and tells us his son, daughter-in-law and grandchildren live in Dallas, but he only gets to see them a couple of times a year. He decided to stay put in his house during the storm even though there was a mandatory evacuation because he likes being in his own place.

"I don't have anyone else to look after since my wife Jasmine passed away a few years ago," he says.

Before he leaves, mom gives Mr. McEwan a plate of chocolate chip cookies and promises to send us and Bertram over to visit him during our neighborhood walks.

We are thrilled to have our pet back home.

Chapter 20

Back to School

It feels like we were on Christmas break without the gifts once we return to school. We haven't seen most of our classmates for two whole weeks, and I've forgotten many of the lessons we've been studying. Thankfully, our teachers say they are going to ease us back into our subjects rather than piling the work on as they do after other long holidays, since some kids are still flooded out of their homes and living in hotels or with relatives.

"I brought Mr. Toad with us to Austin during the storm, and I got lots of great data," says Nathan Jones, hurrying down the hall to the science lab, gripping his mason jar and goggles. "I just need to do one more test with him and I'll be finished."

Leave it to Nathan to keep working even when we don't have to.

Throughout the break I've kept in touch with Chloe and Mariama by text, so they know Valentina taught me all the tryout cheers.

"It will be so cool if we all make the squad together!" enthuses Chloe. "I've been practicing all break."

"Me too," says Mariama. "It was a good way to keep my mind off the storm when the water rose to our front door."

"Valentina!" we squeal and give her a hug when she arrives near our lockers.

"Hola!"

I see she is wearing a new school uniform and has a new backpack too. "The PTA gave me clothes and school supplies," she whispers to me off to the side.

We plan to meet up in the gym during lunchtime to practice our cheers. The one-day cheer clinic and tryouts for the squad will start on Wednesday. Mom actually seemed excited when I told her I was trying out for the squad.

"Since you're not on a sports team, this will be a way to keep you active," she said.

I'm nervous on the second day of the clinic Thursday afternoon, which is our performance day. Though I feel confident in doing the cheer motions, I've only ever done them in front of my friends, and not a crowd of people. From what I hear, most everyone makes the team at our school because it's so small, unless they have bad grades or behavior problems, or are just totally uncoordinated. But I heard that the coach usually limits the squad to ten girls, and there are twelve of us trying out. I hope I don't fall during my cartwheel, or slip up on the gym floor.

It doesn't help that some boys are on the other side of the gym playing basketball while we are stretching.

"Get used to it ladies," says the cheer coach Ms. Christie, when she sees a few of us glaring at the players. "The boys' team will often be working out in the gym the same time we are because of limited space."

Chloe does her practice routine perfectly, and looks so cute sliding into her splits. Mariama follows, and she also performs like an old pro. Since Valentina is cheer captain, she doesn't have to do the routine and has been helping us new girls learn.

"Next up is Sophie Washington," says Ms. Christie glancing at her clipboard.

I move to the front of the group with confidence. Inside I'm shaking, but I follow my dad's advice to fake it 'til you make when trying something that's challenging.

Boom Chicka Boom!
Shake the Room!

I begin loudly, then I see movement out of the corner of my eye.

"Somebody catch him, please!" Nathan is rushing across they gym with his mason jar again, and Mr. Toad is making a beeline straight toward me.

Rockets Got That Zoom Zoom Zoom!

I swing my hips, while the frog leaps on, then off, my head, and my friends stare, aghast.

We will get the win tonight!

Come on Rockets, Fight, Fight, Fight!

I end the cheer in a perfect cartwheel, and view Nathan on the other side of the gym popping the lid back on the jar over his frog. I want to run under the bleachers and hide I'm so embarrassed, but then Valentina starts to cheer.

"Woo hoo! Way to go, Sophie! That was awesome!"

"Yeah, Sophie! Alright!" yell Chloe and Mari-ama, doing herky cheer jumps. We leave tryouts linking arms and praying that we all make the squad.

My hands are sweaty Friday morning as we rush to the gym to check out the cheer team list. Second on the page is my name, Ms. Sophie Washington!

"Congratulations, ladies, you all made it!" says Ms. Christie, coming up behind us. "We had so many great girls trying out that I decided not to limit the squad to just ten this year and included all twelve."

"Yay!" We gather for a group hug. I never thought I'd want to be a cheerleader but this is going to be fun.

Four weeks later, I wave at Mom, Dad and Cole in the stands and hit the floor for our first home basketball game. Valentina, Mariama, Chloe and I line up in formation with our squad members to begin our cheer, happy to be back in our normal routines after the storm and together again with our friends.

We're gonna win tonight!

We're gonna score tonight!

We're gonna take it down the floor tonight!

Oh yes, we've said it before, and now we'll say it again.

The Xavier Rockets team is here to win!

Go Rockets!

Valentina's
Spanish Dictionary

Abuela - Grandmother

Adiós - Goodbye

Churro -A deep-fried pastry sprinkled with sugar, similar to a donut or fritter.

De nada - You're welcome. It's nothing.

Dios - God

Familia - Family

Hola - Hi. Hello

Muy - Very

Vámanos - Let's go

Dear Reader:

Thank you for reading *Sophie Washington: Hurricane*. I hope you liked it. If you enjoyed the book, I'd be grateful if you post a short review on Amazon. Your feedback really makes a difference and helps others learn about my books.

I appreciate your support!

Tonya Duncan Ellis

Books by
Tonya Duncan Ellis

For information on all Tonya Duncan Ellis books about Sophie and her friends

Check out the following pages!

You'll find:

* Blurbs about the other exciting books in the Sophie Washington series

* Information about Tonya Duncan Ellis

Sophie Washington: Queen of the Bee

Sign up for the spelling bee?

No way!

If there's one thing 10-year-old Texan Sophie Washington is good at, it's spelling. She's earned straight 100s on all her spelling tests to prove it. Her parents want her to compete in the Xavier Academy spelling bee, but Sophie wishes they would buzz off.

Her life in the Houston suburbs is full of adventures, and she doesn't want to slow down the action. Where else can you chase wild hogs out of your yard, ride a bucking sheep, or spy an eight-foot-long alligator during a bike ride through the neighborhood? Studying spelling words seems as fun as getting stung by a hornet, in comparison.

That's until her irritating classmate, Nathan Jones, challenges her. There's no way she can let Mr. Know-It-All win. Studying is hard when you have a pesky younger brother and a busy social calendar. Can Sophie ignore the distractions and become Queen of the Bee?

Sophie Washington: The Snitch

There's nothing worse than being a tattletale...

That's what 10-year-old Sophie Washington thinks until she runs into Lanie Mitchell, a new girl at school. Lanie pushes Sophie and her friends around at their lockers, and even takes their lunch money.

If they tell, they are scared the other kids in their class will call them snitches and won't be their friends. And when you're in the fifth grade, nothing seems worse than that.

Excitement at home keeps Sophie's mind off the trouble with Lanie.

She takes a fishing trip to the Gulf of Mexico with her parents and little brother, Cole, and discovers a mysterious creature in the attic above her room. For a while, Sophie is able to keep her parents from knowing what is going on at school. But Lanie's bullying goes too far, and a classmate gets seriously hurt. Sophie needs to make a decision. Should she stand up to the bully, or become a snitch?

Sophie Washington: Things You Didn't Know About Sophie

Oh, the tangled web we weave...

Sixth grader Sophie Washington thought she had life figured out when she was younger, but this school year, everything changed. She feels like an outsider because she's the only one in her class without a cell phone, and her crush, new kid Toby Johnson, has been calling her best friend Chloe. To fit in, Sophie changes who she is. Her plan to become popular works for a while, and she and Toby start to become friends.

In between the boy drama, Sophie takes a whirlwind class field trip to Austin, TX, where she visits the state museum, eats Tex-Mex food, and has a wild ride on a kayak. Back at home, Sophie fights off buzzards from her family's roof, dissects frogs in science class, and has fun at her little brother Cole's basketball tournament.

Things get more complicated when Sophie "borrows" a cell phone and gets caught. If her parents make her tell the truth, what will her friends think? Turns out Toby has also been hiding something, and Sophie discovers the best way to make true friends is to be yourself.

Sophie Washington: The Gamer

40 Days Without Video Games? Oh No!

Sixth-grader Sophie Washington and her friends are back with an interesting book about having fun with video games while keeping balance. It's almost Easter, and Sophie and her family get ready to start fasts for Lent with their church, where they give up doing something for 40 days that may not be good for them. Her parents urge Sophie to stop tattling so much and encourage her second-grade brother Cole to give up something he loves most, playing video games. The kids agree to the challenge, but how long can they keep it up? Soon after Lent begins, Cole starts sneaking to play his video games. Things start to get out of control when he loses a school electronic tablet he checked out without his parents' permission and comes to his sister for help. Should Sophie break her promise and tattle on him?

Sophie Washington: Hurricane

#Sophie Strong

A hurricane's coming, and eleven-year-old Sophie Washington's typical middle school life in the Houston, Texas suburbs is about to make a major change. One day she's teasing her little brother, Cole, dodging classmate Nathan Jones' wayward science lab frog and complaining about "braggamuffin" cheerleader Valentina Martinez, and the next, she and her family are fleeing for their lives to avoid dangerous flood waters. Finding a place to stay isn't easy during the disaster, and the Washington's get some surprise visitors when they finally do locate shelter. To add to the trouble, three members of the Washington family go missing during the storm, and new friends lose their home. In the middle of it all, Sophie learns to be grateful for what she has and that she is stronger than she ever imagined.

Sophie Washington: Mission Costa Rica

Welcome to the Jungle

Sixth grader Sophie Washington, her good friends, Chloe and Valentina, and her parents and brother, Cole, are in for a week of adventure when her father signs them up for a Spring Break mission trip to Costa Rica. Sophie has dreams of lazing on the beach under palm trees, but these are squashed quicker than an underfoot banana once they arrive in the rain forest and are put to work, hauling buckets of water, painting and cooking. Near the hut they sleep in, the girls fight off wayward iguanas and howler monkeys, and nightly visits from a surprise "guest" make it hard for them to get much rest after their work is done.

A wrong turn in the jungle, midway through the week, makes Sophie wish she could leave South America and join another classmate who is doing a Spring Break vacation in Disney World.

In between the daily chores the family has fun times zip lining through the rain forest and taking an exciting river cruise in crocodile-filled waters. Sophie meets new friends during the mission week who show her a different side of life, and by the end of the trip, she starts to see Costa Rica as a home away from home.

About the Author

Tonya Duncan Ellis feels blessed that her home wasn't flooded by Hurricane Harvey as many in her community were affected by this natural disaster. She lives in the suburbs of Houston, TX with her husband and three children. *Sophie Washington: Hurricane* is the fifth book in her Sophie Washington book series, which includes: *Queen of the Bee, The Snitch, Things You Didn't Know About Sophie* and *The Gamer.*